Widows Ridge

By Steven Paul Watson

Widows Ridge

Published by Steven Paul Watson

ISBN-13: 979-8-218-38502-6

Visit the author at: www.stevenpaulwatson.com.

Available in eBook and paperback.

With many special thanks to everyone who has supported me through this ride so far. To those who are persistently interested in my work and always encouraging me to keep moving forward. Thank you!

Works By Steven Paul Watson

Widows Ridge

Fairywood Falls

Howling Moon Series:

Howling Moon: The Beginning

Full Wolf Moon

Other Works:

Human 76 (Anthology Entry "The Hunted")

Table of Contents:

Chapter One

Dustin McCoy wasn't superstitious, but there was always something about the mountains of Eastern Kentucky in that first hour after the sun set that made the hairs on the back of his neck stand. He was a few months past his twenty-third birthday, and he felt silly about how scared he was. That was what made him stop and stare intently at the old fence line, just the odd feeling that he was being watched, and it was one intuition his grandpa had always told him not to ignore. Often, there was something there he just couldn't see, his grandpa would insist. A deer, or a squirrel, or the old bog witch of Letcher County. The bog witch of Letcher

County was his grandpa's favorite tale to tell around a campfire, even when Dustin and his cousins were no older than five, and the old man knew it was going to give them nightmares about an old crone that would pluck the eyes out of children and eat them.

Dustin knew his eyes had to be playing tricks on him, leaning forward, watching the small stand of trees just beyond the rustic barrier. He thought he saw a woman standing there, but the light was so dim it had to have all been his mind playing tricks on him. With as many ghost stories the old timers had fed him as a kid, it was no wonder he anxiously scratched at the raw spot on the back of his hand. A nervous tick he had developed in high school, and he'd been doing it more often of late since he'd proposed to his girlfriend, Amber. He clutched his wrist when he realized he was doing it. He glanced down at the broken skin that he had finally gotten healed enough so it would stop bleeding to see the small scabs had once again broken free and trickles of blood were beading up on his hand.

"Shit," he mumbled to himself, wiping his hand against his jeans and holding the pressure there in hopes it would stop swiftly.

He again looked to the stand of trees, hoping to see the old crone there pointing at him with her ancient fingers, but there was nothing. So many fables and ghost stories about the mountains, one after the other, seemed even more far-fetched than the last. But all had a common theme, don't go outside after dark.

"Hey," he heard his friend call out from behind him. "You okay down there?"

"Yeah, be there in just a sec," he replied as he situated himself and zipped his jeans back up, taking another look in the direction of where he thought he had seen the woman.

He waited for a few more moments, just watching, clinging to the hope he wasn't completely losing his mind before he turned. But he wondered what he would do if he wasn't crazy, and there really was some old crone there wanting to eat his eyeballs. He turned with a laugh, heading back up the embankment, still holding pressure on the back of his hand into his old flannel shirt. He took a deep breath, and the smell of honeysuckle was stronger than before. He hadn't noticed it until then.

Dustin reached the top of the embankment, where his best friend had been sitting. He turned, looking out into the distance. The sun had been down for a while, but the sky still had that mysterious light blue tint that could almost make you think the sun was going to peek out from behind one of the roaming dark clouds. He watched how swiftly the clouds moved through the sky, traveling in and out of the mountain range just as the bright full moon peaked out to greet him, instead shattering any hope of the sun chasing the bog witch away.

He had to admit despite the fear the darkness caused he was going to miss this view. There was nothing quite like the mountains of Harlan County, on the night of a full moon, when there was a chance of a storm, it was the perfect mixture. Everything around him looked as if it was painted on a canvas.

"I can't believe you're marrying that woman in one week!" Dustin broke from his star gazing to look at his companion. His friend was standing close enough to touch with an outstretched hand. Dustin retrieved the beer and quickly opened it. He lifted the bottle to his lips, trying to take in the beauty one more time to etch it into his memory. "Are you even listening to me?"

Jacob was bigger than him in every way, taller and heavier, though not in an overweight way. Dustin was finding the bottom of the bottle when he glanced at Jacob, who was busy fiddling with his phone.

He wasn't sure if it was his fifth or sixth, not that it really mattered. The entire purpose of the hunting trip was to catch up with his best friend and soon-to-be best man. It was a plus that he planned on getting absolutely trashed. The chance to go out and hunt was just an excuse they used to make the trip happen. Often, that was how their hunting trips turned out; the two of them passed out with the dogs waking them up in the morning.

Dustin couldn't remember the last time he'd gotten good and drunk; it was no doubt before he started dating Amber. Just the thought of his soon-to-be wife made him smile despite his friend being so obscenely opposed to the union.

"I just can't believe it, man. What the hell do you even see in her?"

He was beginning to regret asking Jacob to be his best man. Dustin tossed the bottle into the back of the side-by-side and glared at the other man who was doing much the same as him. He and Jacob Gardner had been friends since kindergarten; they had bloodied each other's noses fighting over building blocks, and they had been best of friends ever since.

Dustin looked around, pausing when he thought he saw someone standing in the shadows of the tree line once again. He lowered his head to get a better look and could no longer find what had caught his eye. This time, it was a spot a little further up the hill from where he had last thought he'd seen the figure. He wanted to bring it to his friend's attention, but when he glanced at Jacob, he was busy bringing another drink of his own.

Maybe he had more beers than he thought. He tried to concentrate on the area but saw nothing moving, and he glanced at the moon, which was mostly hidden behind an intricate webbing of clouds littering the skies. It added to the eerie feeling he was being watched. He heard Jacob grumble something he couldn't quite make out and took a deep breath, for some reason feeling like he should put a harsh tone on what he was going to say, "She's your sister."

"Exactly, I know how bat shit crazy she is, man. You don't realize just how off her rocker she is yet," Jacob said with a hearty laugh, and Dustin could tell he was serious about his future bride, which made him a little angry.

He'd known the two siblings for most of their life. Before high school, the two used to fight like cats and dogs. And there were times after Jacob made it into high school that it was much worse. He often wondered if it was jealousy on one or the other's part. But he never stepped in, even when there were times he thought he should have. Jacob wouldn't admit it, but there were even times Amber had gotten the better of him.

"I've been with Amber going on three years," Dustin felt like he needed to interject. They had started dating shortly after she had graduated from high school. The attraction was there before, but he was three years older than her, and he felt weird about it being anything but friendship. "If she could hear you now," Dustin twisted the top off his next victim, tossing the cap into the darkness with a snap of his finger, a whistle, and then a clang as it bounced off something neither of them could see.

Click, click, click.

Dustin paused at the sound for a moment. It would almost pass as an echo, except it didn't sound like something metal bouncing.

"I know what she'd do," Jacob said with a less confident laugh. "She'd shoot my ass. Like I said, she's crazy, and three years isn't nearly long enough for you to realize how much so."

"I've known your sister nearly as long as I've known you, Jacob," he hissed out his frustration at his soon-to-be brother-in-law.

"Yeah, but you've not lived with her nearly as long as I have," Jacob responded. Truthfully, he had only lived with his fiancé for a few months despite their long commitment to each other.

There was a long silence between the two of them as he watched the darkness, his eyes drawn back in the direction he'd seen the figure earlier, convincing himself despite his persistent looking for the shadow, it was his imagination running wild. There was no bog witch there to get him. He was no longer a child… and Letcher County was quite a ways away.

"Be honest with me. Your dad acts differently around me now. Does he hate me?" Dustin questioned before he took another drink. He found himself looking forward at the ground, almost wanting to avoid the answer.

Jacob laughed. His laugh was so loud that if there had been anything nearby watching, it would have scurried off in fear at his friend's hyena-like laugh. Or come closer to inspect a potential meal.

"Seriously, Dad wants her out of that house more than anybody," Jacob replied, and the two of them laughed in unison as they gave a clanking toast with their beer bottles. "But seriously, I cannot believe you're actually going to marry her."

"Shush," he said with a smile. "I'm being serious, though; your mom loves me. Even more so than she does you and Amber… but your dad scares me a bit. He's been acting differently since Amber, and I got engaged."

"Trust me," Jacob interjected, "I think Dad probably likes you a whole lot more than me most days as well."

"Well, I guess I can understand that" Dustin said before taking another drink.

"So, what are we going to do for your bachelor party?" Jacob questioned.

"No strippers," Dustin said.

"Oh, there is going to be a stripper. Maybe play some cards and get drunk. You sprung this on us so quickly…" There was a pause between the two of them. "Is Amber pregnant?"

His best friend gave him a dead glare. He had never really seen Jacob look so serious. Being sincere about anything was the last thing Jacob ever did. "No." His friend continued to stare at him angrily. "I got a job offer out of Lexington… and I think I'm going to have to take it. Amber is the only other person who knows. I haven't even told my parents that we're moving yet."

"You said job offer and then that you're moving, so you've already accepted the job?" Jacob questioned. Dustin watched his expression change as he looked away from him and toward the ground. He could hear the disappointed huff come from his friend. The two of them had been inseparable since the days of bleeding each other's noses, and neither of them had an abundance of friends.

"I start in a month; the money was too good to pass it by. It's a life-changing opportunity, and I wanted Amber to be a part of that," Dustin said. "I don't mean to make it sound like I'm too good for Harlan. It's just there's nothing for me or her here. When we have kids…" Jacob looked at him with a questioning glare. "She's not pregnant, don't even think that. But when we have kids…we want them to be able to have opportunities we just didn't have growing up here."

"I'm a little jealous." Dustin watched as Jacob took a drink of his beer and then settled in with a deep breath. "Definitely getting a stripper now."

Dustin looked down at his phone to see if the tracking collars were getting closer or farther away, and he couldn't remember just how long it had been, but the dogs hadn't moved. "I think my app is glitching. The dogs haven't moved in nearly twenty minutes."

"I think they've got something," Jacob said, leaning in to get a closer look at the app.

"I don't hear them barking, though. Shouldn't they be barking?" Dustin tossed the now empty bottle into the back with another clang.

"Don't try to change the subject," Jacob replied, pulling a couple more beers from the empty cooler and pushing one into Dustin's chest. "You marry my sister in one week. It's not too late to back out and run like hell. I'm sure even witness protection will probably take you in and get you away from her if you want."

"I'm marrying your sister. She's also the love of my life," he said, trying to put forth a more serious tone. It didn't go unnoticed as Jacob snorted with laughter. "So maybe you should try to be a little bit nicer."

"Hell no. I mean if she'd be a little bit nicer to Dad and me… You don't realize just how mean she can be, and you're going to be spending the rest of your life with the brat," Jacob said, and for a moment, Dustin thought the man was completely serious until his lips twitched into a soft curl of a smile.

"The sex is amazing. That woman is crazy in bed," Dustin replied, and he could see his friend's expression go from that half smile to embarrassment in a few words.

"Hush. I definitely don't want to hear you talk about my sister," Jacob responded as he turned away.

"Yeah, we don't use a bed that often. Usually, it's wherever the mood strikes us, and she does this thing with her mouth…" Dustin said as he took another big drink of beer.

"Shut up, please. We didn't bring nearly enough beer for this." Now Jacob was the one looking at the phone. "You're right. They haven't moved in twenty minutes."

Chapter Two

Dustin stood looking at the phone held in front of him. His mind was still on the clearing and the shadows that had plagued his mind with childhood horrors. "How close are we to Berkley Branch?"

"I don't know, a couple miles away, I think." Jacob turned in his spot, looking around to see if he might be able to give a more accurate account of where they were. Dustin watched as he circled, cracked open another beer, and started drinking it. He threw the top off into the darkness. There was a long pause between the two of them. Dustin was listening for the strange echo he had heard from the last bottle cap he'd tossed into the darkness.

"Are you sure we're that far away?" Dustin glanced toward his friend and then back to the clearing just as the moon broke through the clouds again, lighting up a small cluster of bushes near him and the spiderweb that had taken over a nearby tree.

"Are you afraid of some fairy tale our parents used to squawk about the old mansion up Berkley Branch? You don't believe those stories, do you? You know how crazy that is."

"You know how nuts it is someone still lives up in that holler. They ate people up in there," Dustin said, his heart beginning to race a bit with just the thought of being that close to something that had haunted them since they were children.

He remembered when he was a sophomore in high school, a bunch of his classmates skipped school just to drive up Berkley Branch, and he had refused. The stories still stuck with him. At least once a year, he would have very vivid nightmares about being stuck in a house with a cannibal after him chasing him down the stairs into a cramped, dark basement, and then he would wake up. He started to scratch at the back of his hand until he noticed Jacob was watching him, and he abruptly quit.

"No, they didn't. Just the one woman paralyzed her husband or some odd stuff like that. I don't really believe any of it, never have. They just wanted to scare us so we wouldn't go up in there," Jacob said. Dustin couldn't recall if Jacob was one of those who had gone on the trip their sophomore year, but Dustin highly doubted Jacob would have gone without him.

He felt like that little kid on the playground trying to convince others of a far-fetched story his parents had told him. He did everything but stomp his feet, but when he went to argue with his longtime friend, nothing came out. He just returned to glaring at the map he had pulled up on his phone.

"The truth is, some sort of hippie pagan witch or something lived in that mansion, and they were afraid she would be a bad influence on our impressionable minds. If our parents only knew half of what we used to get into when we went out at night, they would have shipped us off to military school or some private catholic school. But then they had no clue what all those stuffy church kids got into when they all went out after Sunday service, either. There were even rumors that the youth pastor worshipped her and fell in love with her. So, I don't think she ate her husband. I think he ran off because he couldn't handle her. There were also the stories about Orgies and wild parties she used to throw."

"I think she ate him," Dustin quickly replied, ignoring the crudeness of Jacob's version of the holler.

"Listen to yourself a little bit. You're marrying my sister, and you're talking about a woman who ate people all right here in Harlen County. You know how crazy that sounds," Jacob replied. "Maybe you're getting cold feet."

"I heard some stories about what went on up there during the Civil War, how the women of that house always look so eerily the same. Some even went as far as to say that it is the same woman, and she's been alive up in there since the time of the settlers in this area," Dustin said with a laugh. It wasn't a real laugh, as he was trying to sound more confident than he was as he scanned the darkness for anyone who might have been watching them.

"You've been visiting my grandmother, haven't you?" Jacob said with a laugh. "She's the only person that I know that has been telling that version of the story. She even claims that she knew her way back in the days of running moonshine when Harlan was a dry county and some shit like that. Like they even have the same scar up under her chin, claiming she was stabbed by one of her many victims. You really shouldn't be listening to her; she's got onset dementia."

"Well, your grandmother is a saint, and you should go spend more time with her. Especially if you believe she is losing her mind like you're trying to say," Dustin said. "And when Amber and I are gone, it would be good for the both of you. I know she misses seeing you."

"You're right. I should go see her more." Jacob lowered his head for a moment. "How about the stories of a giant spider-like creature?" There was laughter in Jacob's voice, and Dustin had tried to stop himself, but he snorted out a laugh of his own.

"That one might not be true," he responded, his stomach starting to hurt from holding back his laughter.

There was a long pause between the two of them as the wind began to pick up. "Looks like it may actually rain," Dustin said, looking off in the distance. "Maybe we should call the dogs back."

"You are really scared of going over in that holler, aren't you?" Jacob said as he pulled a whistle out of his jacket pocket.

"Honestly, yes," Dustin said as he took another glance at his phone. "Whether the stories are real or not, I really don't want to go over in that place."

Jacob hit the whistle, and they sat and listened but heard nothing from the two dogs. Normally, they would bark if they were close enough to hear the whistle. "Damn," Jacob muttered, putting it back into his pocket.

"Maybe if we stay up high and cross over into the holler just a bit and try the whistles again," Dustin replied. He looked at his friend, whose complexion was a bit pale. "I'm certain it is Berkley Branch." Dustin took the final drink of his beer and tossed the bottle into the collection before jumping off the side-by-side.

"Come on, let's go get some dogs and go home. I need to see your sister," he said with a laugh, trying to come across as a bit braver than he was feeling. "She's going to do that thing with her mouth." Dustin took a moment to check the pistol in the holster on his hip.

"Shut up. I don't want to know what my sister does with her mouth," Jacob quickly grabbed the spotlights and a shotgun from the case in the back of the side-by-side.

The two of them walked about a hundred feet around the hill in the direction the app was showing the collar's location, not stopping until they reached an old, rickety wood fence line. "Try the whistle again," Dustin said, trying not to sound as scared as he was. He realized they had passed by where the shadows had convinced him he'd seen someone, but it was the same old fence they were following.

He watched as Jacob pulled the whistle from his pocket, gave it two quick blows, and listened. They heard nothing but silence as the wind cut around them, making the leaves on the trees move. "Even the air feels colder over here. I should have brought my jacket." He was regretting coming at all now, thinking only about getting someplace safe, far, far away from Berkley Branch.

Click, click, click.

Dustin stood staring off into the darkness, certain he heard the sound clearly this time and knew it wasn't an echo of any sort. All the stories that he had been told about Widow's Ridge as a kid came flooding back to him. How they scared him to death and would keep him up late at night. Again, he heard it. The distinctive sound of something clicking somewhere high above him caused the hairs on the back of his neck to stand.

Chapter Three

Click *click, click.*

The sound of a limb recoiling off the wooden fence caught his attention as he placed a hand on the top run. It had been a long time since the fence had new runners, and it felt like it might crumble under his touch.

"Can we just get this over with?" Jacob sounded as out of it as Dustin was. But there was one thing he knew about Jacob; he would never admit to being scared.

Dustin stepped up to the old unstable fence, placing a foot on the bottom, and slung his other leg up. He heard the wood snap under his weight, sending him toppling over into a mix of mud and leaves. He heard Jacob laughing as he glanced back at him angrily.

"It's not funny," he muttered mostly to himself. If the situation had been reversed, he had no doubt he would have laughed as well, but, at that moment, all he could think about was how much he wanted to be anywhere else. Dustin stood dusting himself off before picking his light up just in time to see Jacob walk through where the fence had just broken the moment before. Dustin sighed.

Click, click, click.

He had heard the sound again, a little further away from the first time before his unfortunate tumble. This time, it sounded more intent and somewhere in the trees around the hill from them. "Did you hear that?" Dustin questioned, shining his light in the direction of the sound.

"Hear what?" He glanced back at Jacob, who was checking his phone. He hoped he was looking at the app for the collars but wasn't entirely sure.

"A tapping sound… I think," Dustin wasn't quite sure what it was he heard as he grumbled to himself, feeling like he was going crazy, letting the old ghost stories get to him. He took a couple quick steps forward with the light shining out in front and stopped swiftly, so fast he heard Jacob come to a staggering stop behind him.

"Hey, watch it. A little warning next time," Jacob proclaimed.

Dustin looked back at him and then back to the obstacle in his path. *Spider's web.* Dustin reached down and grabbed a small stick, placing it on one of the pilot lines of the web, and gave it a tug, watching the water fall from the silk. "Check this out," he said, "Have you ever seen a spiderweb like this?"

Jacob came up beside him, and Dustin watched as his friend placed his finger in the webbing. "I've never seen web that..."

"Thick, right?" Dustin gritted his teeth.

The two of them seemed to stare at each other for an uncomfortable minute before Dustin broke from the gaze.

Jacob took a stick of his own, knocked the web out of the way, and stepped forward, taking the lead around the hill. Dustin stood back, looking down the holler, where, for a moment, he thought he'd seen something move. The sound of Jacob swearing inaudibly brought him back to reality. His friend was thrashing out at the darkness in front of him.

"What is it?" Dustin questioned.

"I walked right into one of those thick ass spiderwebs. For a second there, I thought I knew what a fly felt like walking into that horror. It's much stronger than it looks." Dustin watched as Jacob pulled it off his face and flung it away. Now Dustin was the one laughing.

"I hate freaking spiders," Jacob proclaimed.

"Bandit!" Dustin yelled out.

"A little warning next time before you yell like that, I almost messed myself," Jacob said, looking back.

"Bandit!" Dustin yelled again. "Come on, boy, time to go home."

"If you're moving to Lexington, what are you going to do with Bandit?" Jacob turned his full body, leaning on the walking stick he'd acquired in one hand and the shotgun in the other.

"Guess he's about to become an expensive house dog," Dustin replied.

"Roscoe!" Jacob yelled, giving a shout for his own dog. "Let's go."

Dustin pulled out his phone and quickly scanned through the app. "Collar shows are still up there somewhere."

"They haven't moved. They must have found something to eat or..." Jacob nodded, looking out through the darkness.

"Or something's wrong." Dustin's heart raced. He always thought it odd to have a dog for a specific purpose. Most of the pets he had through his youth were much more than work dogs. "Bandit!" he yelled again, his voice cracking.

"We would have heard something if something was wrong. We weren't that far away," Jacob reassured him. "They have something up a tree, and they're just sitting on it. Bobcat, maybe?"

"Or one of those damn panther's your grandmother goes on about," Dustin replied.

"There are no panthers or mountain lions in Eastern Kentucky," Jacob again turned to face him. "Wish people would quit talking that stuff. And I thought we already cleared up the fact my grandmother isn't playing with a full deck?"

"Come on, Bandit!" Dustin yelled again. Again, no answer. "Let's go home," he said no more than a whisper.

Both started walking again. Dustin veered up the hill away from Jacob this time and instantly regretted it, walking directly into a spiderweb. "This shit is everywhere," he proclaimed as he pulled it off his face and neck. He spat into the darkness, feeling as if he had gotten something in his mouth, which he didn't want to know. He shook his hair violently, trying to get anything that may have been there hanging in the web free from his hair.

Jacob didn't have to ask what. "I know I still feel it in my hair as well. It's so sticky."

The two of them walked a dozen more steps, "Bandit, Roscoe!" they both called out in unison. No reply from the dogs.

"Maybe we should come back in the morning when we can actually see where we're going," Jacob said. "I'm sure they'll be okay until morning."

"I'm not," Dustin mumbled, watching Jacob climb the hill to get on the same level as him. He didn't want to admit it, and the last thing he wanted to do was express his fear out loud, but he didn't think they were going to find the dogs.

Jacob yelled again, "Here, Roscoe. I got a bone for you!" Jacob looked back at him, "They're here somewhere. We'll find them. I promise I'll get you back to my sister if you don't tell her all the stuff I was talking about her, that is."

"I won't," he said with a laugh, "not today, anyways, but you know next week we're going to visit your grandmother. We might have that conversation then, and I'll have you deal with both at once. Or just bring it all up at the wedding itself."

"At which point I tell my very Christian family that it's a shotgun wedding, y'all are pregnant, and see how all of that goes down," Jacob replied. If it had been a Western, it was just a matter of moments before they'd draw their guns and fire. There was a long pause between the two of them, only broken when they both heard dogs barking off in the distance, causing them to look away.

"That sounded like Bandit," Dustin said as he pulled his phone from his pocket, and the signal from the collars hadn't moved. "But that's way out over there. You don't think they slipped their collars?"

"Those collars are expensive," Jacob replied. Dustin watched as he walked on in the direction of the collars.

"I wish the moon would come out from behind those clouds." He looked away from his stomping friend to the sky; he could see some of it through the clouds, but it wasn't casting much light. Again, a dog barked in the distance. "That's definitely Bandit," Dustin grumbled to himself.

"I haven't heard Roscoe," Jacob said, shining the light back in Dustin's eyes. "He may be up here with the collars.

"Roscoe has never been what you'd call the barker. Maybe he's with Bandit," Dustin stated, but he knew it was unlikely that both dogs would have slipped their collars in the same spot.

"It's fine. Those collars can be replaced," Jacob said as he began to move off toward the ridge, away from where the collar signal was but in the direction of the barking dogs.

They moved about twenty feet before Dustin was again hit in the face by a spiderweb and started swatting away like a mad person, smacking the stick he had acquired on the ground all around him. "How many spiders are in this holler?" he cursed.

"I hope you can be prepared for killing spiders the rest of your life," Jacob said with a laugh, and when Dustin was finally finished swatting at the darkness, he looked at his best friend and gave him a finger. "My sister hates the damn things."

"I didn't think I had a fear of them, but I'm having a sudden onset of arachnophobia with all of the web." Dustin laughed out with frustration. "This isn't natural; it's winter, and I've never seen such a concentration of spiderwebs in one general area in all my life. Shouldn't they be in like a freaking hibernation, a cocoon, or some shit... what is it spiders do in the winter, anyway?" Dustin watched as Jacob looked away back in the direction they'd come. "What is it?"

"I thought I heard something," Jacob replied.

Dustin hadn't, but he had been too busy swatting in the darkness. He slowly put his hand out into the darkness, trying to pull the remaining silk off his face. "What was it?"

"My imagination is going a bit wild at the moment," Jacob replied.

Dustin sighed. He had been so focused on listening for the dogs and battling the spiderweb he had forgotten the figure he'd seen in the clearing and the odd sounds. He looked around. "Are we going crazy?"

"Long past, I'd say," Jacob replied.

"Come on, Dustin," Jacob swerved to start heading straight up the hill, and Dustin rushed to catch up. "I'm not going down any further. Let's get back out of here."

The dogs barked again; this time, they had moved back in the direction of the collars. Dustin could hear Jacob continue to walk, and he tried to gather himself until he heard his friend stop. "We're still going after them, aren't we?"

"You're the one who said there was nothing to be afraid of, and listen, they're getting closer," Dustin answered.

Dustin led the way. They walked toward the ridge but kept a pace around the hill in the direction the collars were. "Maybe we should invest in some sort of glow-in-the-dark collars or something."

"I just realized this may be our last hunt," Jacob said, and Dustin realized he'd quit walking.

"Now you're just being melodramatic. Let's get these dogs and head home," Dustin said as he glanced at his phone and looked at the map. "They should be somewhere right around there." Dustin pointed into the darkness, and by the app, they were within a couple hundred feet of them. Dustin took a couple of steps forward and realized Jacob was being quiet, too quiet, and he glanced back at his friend shining the light in his direction. He half expected to see him taking a piss or even sitting down, but instead, Jacob just stood there motionless with a blank expression on his face. But most of all, his complexion was ghostly white. "Don't play games with me right now." He highly doubted he was.

"I'm not," Jacob replied.

"Then what is it?" Dustin questioned.

"I thought I heard something again. This time, it was circling us," Jacob answered.

"Bear, maybe?" Dustin began to shine his light off all around them.

"I'm sure it's nothing," Jacob looked at him, and the moment their eyes met, Dustin knew he was lying. He had never seen his friend afraid; in fact, he didn't think he was afraid of anything, but he was terrified now.

"We can go back to the side-by-side," Dustin said.

"No, let's get our dogs," Jacob replied. Dustin didn't move until his friend did; he could see him hesitate, and he took a moment to gather himself before he followed along. They walked a couple dozen steps before both stopped immediately, looking at each other. They had both heard it this time. Somewhere in front of them, a limb snapped under the weight of something moving and a scramble in the underbrush.

Dustin slowly brought his light up. "Do you see anything?"

"No," he heard Jacob whisper, but he heard him drop the stick, and he imagined his friend now holding the shotgun to his shoulder.

A crack of a limb. "It's a deer. It must be a deer, a bear, or a freaking wild boar. You know the population is starting to boom here. Not that it makes me feel any better."

"It's just a freaking myth about like the Berkley cannibal," Jacob proclaimed.

"Yeah, it's an unsolved mystery until you get a boar's tusk up your ass," Dustin said. He could feel himself starting to hyperventilate on the verge of a panic attack as he shined the light all around.

"Same as I don't want to know what you and my sister do in the bedroom, so you know, keep that to yourself." He could almost see his friend's expression without looking back. It was an attempt to lighten the situation. They both chuckled.

Dustin took a deep breath, scanning his phone again. The collars were still motionless. "They're right over there in the direction of the sound. It's our asshole dogs we're hearing."

Dustin could see Jacob now moving out of the corner of his eye, holding the shotgun up to his shoulder. When Jacob stopped moving, they both looked in the direction of the collars. Nothing. Dustin sighed. "This is crazy. We've lived here our entire lives. There is nothing out there watching us or going to hurt us. Whatever it is more scared of us than we are of it."

"I'm pretty freaking scared," Jacob said. "So much so I think I may have messed myself a moment ago."

Dustin knew his friend wasn't joking. He felt much the same way. He moved another dozen steps forward. This time, he could hear Jacob moving with him at the same pace. Moving so fast gave him a bit more confidence than he had expected; it didn't allow his mind to play tricks on him. Dustin heard the leaves rustling just before him and whispered, "Hello?"

He half expected someone to answer, but there was just an earie silence that sent a cold chill up his back. He glanced back at Jacob. "What do you think?"

"I think we should've not come down here," Jacob replied.

"You may be right," Dustin responded as he looked forward.

The two of them took a few steps forward, and once again, the rustling in the leaves started and a gnawing sound.

"Damn it," Dustin said as he rushed forward. His heart raced as he could hear Jacob coming up behind him. He felt his feet give out from him as he slipped down the hill into a rough thicket, and then he saw the outline of a figure in the moonlight just above him.

If he hadn't fallen, he would have run right over the top of it. He felt Jacob's hand on his shoulder going to help him up. Dustin grabbed the flashlight at his side, tangled in some vines, and he could feel them cut into his wrist as he jerked the light free and shined it toward the figure.

Chapter Four

It was a woman. A very naked woman. Dustin paused, looking at her. The night air was cold, but by the look of her back, she was sweating. She knelt over something, her head moving in a violent manner, her wild-up red hair bobbing suggestively. He was so lost in the visual that he wasn't paying any attention to the sounds. Bones crunching and flesh being torn and a low humming growl like something trying to warn off an intruder from trying to take a morsel of meat. Every other moment there was a sucking sound, and something torn from the flesh.

Her spine could be seen just under her pale skin, and every muscle from her thin waist to her shoulders was almost etched in stone. She had thick hips and thighs, and her rear was almost hypnotic as she swayed in her kneeling position. Dustin glanced back toward Jacob, who had lowered his shotgun and was still watching her.

Crunch.

Dustin glanced back toward the woman as the horrendous sounds continued. "Miss," he said barely more than a whisper.

The woman's head stopped moving abruptly when he spoke. It took Dustin only a moment himself to realize the awful sounds had also stopped. He felt his heart race as the woman's head slowly turned to look back at him. Her head slowly turned while the rest of her body didn't move. He saw the dark red eyes first; they were positioned on her forehead, and they blinked rapidly. He took his foot and pushed off a rotted log at his feet; he realized there were six crimson-red eyes positioned on the woman's face, all blinking in unison as the light splashed across her blood-soaked features.

"Shit," he muttered, realizing the woman wasn't looking at him but something else now, Jacob as he ran away.

Dustin looked at the ground around him and didn't see the pistol he was holding a moment before. As her head twisted, he saw her mouth or where her mouth should have been. Chelicerae extended from where her cheeks should have been, expended from the outside of her lips latched on a bloodied rabbit. He scooted again, this time sliding down the hill from her. His light remained on the ground, pointing in her direction.

He heard Jacob yell for him to come on from the darkness. The woman twisted her body to look in the direction they had come. He got a better look at her body. Completely human. Her breasts were shapely with pert nipples, her collarbone soaked in blood running down between her breasts, even covering them in spots as if she'd showered in it. It was obvious the light had a blinding effect on the woman. She hadn't even looked in his direction, her eyes continuing to blink rapidly. He slowly and as gently as he could move his hand over the ground, looking for the gun. It had to be close by, but he never took his eyes off the woman. His heart raced as he looked her over. She was completely human from the neck down, but he could tell there was something supernaturally strong about her muscles, especially her lower body. Her legs looked abnormal; he could only compare them to a gymnast. He settled once again on her face; her strawberry-blonde hair was matted with sweat and blood, and it hung loosely about her shoulders. The chelicerae extended from her jaw had sharp tips and dripped with blood as she pulled the loose fur of the rabbit apart to expose its pink under the flesh. She opened her mouth, larger than humanly possible, exposing fangs as she bit into the rabbit, jerking her jaw to one side, tearing the flesh, but all the while, those six disturbing eyes looked in the direction Jacob had run. Dustin had no problem imagining the thoughts going through this creature's mind, trying to decide whether it was going to give chase or not. Dustin watched, and he thought he had quit breathing, hoping she would just stay put. He was as frozen as she seemed to be.

"Dustin, where are you?" He heard Jacob yell out, and he saw the expression on the creature's face change and the soft thud of the rabbit's carcass falling to the ground. The woman moved so fast he barely was able to see which way she went. But he knew.

"Run, Jacob, fucking run, she's coming!" he screamed as loud as he could. "Fucking run, man!"

His heart raced as he grabbed the flashlight and shined it over the ground until he saw the shine of his gun. It had been sitting in the muck between him and the mysterious creature. He tried to get back to her feet but couldn't pull his leg free. He glanced to his feet at the light, expecting vines, but what he saw sent a new feeling of dread. Web. He was tangled up in thick, silky webbing. He started to rip at it as he tried to pull his foot free. It was sticky, and his fingers matted together as he slunk them, trying to get it off. Finally, he ran his fingers through the mud, getting the silky material off.

A shrill scream erupted through the darkness. Jacob. He continued to rip and tear until his foot finally pulled free. Without standing, he plucked the gun from the ground and got to his feet just as another horrifying scream erupted from the dark. His hesitation was gone as he turned, heading in the direction of his friend.

Dustin wasn't sure how far they had moved away from where their night had begun, but he was surprised when he got to the ATV so quickly. His chest hurt, and he felt like his heart was going to burst as he placed his hands on his hips and tried to catch his breath.

"Jacob," he muttered as he winced and leaned over his head and began to throb with each beat of his heart. He grabbed at his pocket as he opened the half door of the side-by-side, realizing Jacob was the one who had the keys. "Damn it," he muttered, slamming it forcefully.

Dustin circled back to the rear of the vehicle and shined his light, grabbing the shotgun he had left behind and quickly stuffed his pockets with shells. A gunshot rang off somewhere back in the direction he had come. Had he passed them and not realized it? A second shotgun blast buzzed, and he took a deep breath. Jacob was a good shot, the better of the two of them. Dustin started running in the direction of the commotion. He had taken it a few dozen steps before he found himself once again leaning over, trying to catch his breath.

He finally got his composure and started slowly walking down the trail. "Jacob, can you hear me?" he called out. He wasn't whispering, but he wasn't yelling, either. "Jacob," he said in a raspy tone. Dustin walked a dozen more steps when he repeated himself in a closer-to-normal voice, "Jacob, can you hear me?"

He didn't know what he expected, but a reply from his friend wasn't it. "Jacob," a voice called back out to him somewhere in the darkness in front of him. He brought the shotgun to his shoulder and held the flashlight near the pump action. It wasn't Jacob's voice; it was feminine and hoarse.

Click, click, click.

He swung around to his left ready with his finger on the trigger of the shotgun. "Where you at?" he said a little louder than he'd been talking. "What are you?" He thought about earlier in the night when he'd heard the echo and saw a figure standing in the shadows watching them. "I don't believe you want to hurt us." He was sure Jacob was dead. His heart raced. "We shouldn't have come up here and disturbed your home like we did." He swiftly turned to the direction he had been heading, thinking it would try to sneak up on him.

Chapter Five

Dustin stood there for what seemed like hours, but he knew it was no more than a few minutes before he took a dozen steps forward, even dropping the gun from his shoulder. He had to find Jacob. He could not get off the mountain with some story about a spider-like creature. He paused to shine the light over his shoulder to make sure she wasn't there. *A were-spider…* he smiled, knowing how crazy it sounded even thinking it. His fiancé would never forgive him if he left her older brother on the mountain to die alone. Dustin sighed. How was he going to explain this to Amber? How was he going to tell anyone about what happened? There was no way they would believe him. He took a step backward, the way he had come. What if there were people who knew, who wouldn't think he had lost his mind.

Another gunshot, this one so close he could see the fire come from the shotgun's muzzle. Dustin took off in a sprint. "I'm coming, Jacob!" he yelled. Everything happened so fast. When Dustin ran into Jacob headfirst, the two of them flung about, landing on the ground, and everything scattered, including the guns.

"Jacob," Dustin said. "Where is she?"

Jacob glared at him; it was easy to see he was confused by Dustin's question. Dustin picked up a gun and pushed it into Jacob's arms. "Are we going hunting, buddy?" Dustin looked at him, his eyes glossed over. He shined his light behind them to ensure the creature wasn't there and quickly plucked his gun up before turning his attention back to Jacob. He shined the light on Jacob; he now saw the wounds on his neck. He never spoke, and he stood there. Dustin had seen his friend drunk before, and he resembled that now even though he knew he hadn't drunk near enough alcohol to reach that state. "Where is she?" he questioned again, stepping forward to get a better look at the wound on his neck. "Did she bite you?"

"Huh," Jacob muttered. He started to fall, but Dustin caught him.

"Did she… bite you?" Dustin questioned, even though he already knew the obvious answer. What was going to happen to his best friend, or him for that matter? Was he going to turn into some horrifying spider creature as well? When the thought crossed his mind, he took a step back away from his friend, even raising the gun up halfway so he could easily shoot his best friend at point-blank range if he had to.

"Is Amber with you?" Jacob smiled that goofy, lighthearted smile his friend always seemed to have, and Dustin lowered his gun back to the ground.

Dustin looked around, grabbed Jacob under his arm, and put it over his shoulder. He started dragging him back in the direction of the vehicle, three steps, and the two toppled over once again.

"Shit," Dustin said, rushing back to his feet as he turned to look at Jacob. He could tell his friend's complexion was ghostly white, and the wound on his neck oozed abnormal colored blood. He had a blank look in his eyes as he stared up at the night sky. "Jacob, where are the keys?"

"Keys?" he said as he tried to get up but immediately fell back into the muck.

Dustin knelt and quickly began to pat his jacket and clothing, but he had no keys. "They're in the back of the side-by-side…" Dustin stood up straight, grabbed Jacob by the arm, and pulled him along to a standing position. He watched as Jacob put a hand on his neck and looked at his hand. "She bit me."

"We have to get out of here," Dustin said as he picked up the shotgun. "Can you walk?"

"I think I can," Jacob replied.

"We've got to get off this mountain and get you to a hospital," he replied.

"What are we to tell people?" Jacob questioned.

"Doesn't matter, we just need to get off this hill," Dustin said as he stepped around Jacob back in the direction they had run into each other, and he shined a light down the narrow path they had been following.

Dustin turned back and stopped instantly, seeing the woman standing directly behind Jacob. Dustin didn't hesitate. He brought the gun to his shoulder, and for a moment, he saw the confusion on Jacob's face just before he pulled the trigger.

Before he could even wrench another shell in, she had pushed her way past Jacob and knocked Dustin to his back. He twisted away from her, rushing to his feet, and took off down the hill away from her. Dustin didn't know where it was he was going; he just knew he couldn't stop. He couldn't look back. He barreled his way down the hill toward Berkley Hollow. He realized now all those stories he had been told as a child were real and so much more horrifying than he could have imagined. He didn't know how far he had run as he tried to keep the light out in front of him. He didn't see the log about knee high until it was too late, clipping his leg and sending him head over heels into the brush ahead, losing his light in the tumble. His entire body hurt from the fall, or maybe it was because of all the running. He pushed himself onto his elbows, looking back to see the light a few paces away. He slowly twisted until he was on his stomach and crawled to the light. As he took hold of it and turned, the light settled on the woman sitting in a kneeling position on a limb ten feet up in a nearby tree.

She was covered in more blood now; he was completely unsure where all the blood came from. When he had pulled the trigger, he wasn't entirely sure if he hit the woman he'd been aiming at or Jacob, who looked in complete shock at seeing his friend aim a gun at him. He wanted to scream out for his lost friend... but he was scared.

Terrified at the spider-like creature now looking around for its next meal. Then Dustin realized. She didn't see him. He stayed perfectly still, trying not even to breathe as she stood straight up with one hand on the side of the tree. She leaped into the darkness behind the tree, and Dustin lay there a moment, hearing rumbling coming from somewhere in the dark.

He wasn't sure how long he would stay there. An hour maybe, he started to tremble as he reached forward to the light. He picked it up and sat up on his knees, trying to catch his breath. He slowly stood at his feet and started to move again. This time trying to be quieter. Watching every step, he took as he went downward. He had to find his way out eventually, as long as he kept moving down.

Dustin kept the slow, steady pace, ensuring he watched every step he took, even sitting at the base of a large oak tree. He turned the light off and pulled the hood of his jacket over his head. He wrapped his arms across his chest, setting his back firm against the large, solid surface. He took a deep breath, trying to make any noise. He needed to rest; he was exhausted. He tightened his grip across his body as his arms began to shake, followed shortly after by his entire body trembling. It wasn't the cold; he knew he was going into some sort of state of shock as he took a deep breath.

He listened, hearing something stalking through the growth somewhere behind the large tree. His legs began to shake as he tried to hide his face inside his jacket. It was getting closer to circling him. He imagined it was tracking his scent as he tried hard to picture the creature's face. *Did she even have a nose?*

He took a stuttering breath, searching for his phone even though he knew it was long gone, just like the pistol and the shotgun. He sat there with his face hidden until the crackling of the leaves and brush stopped.

Shoosh.

The all-too-familiar sound of a deer snorting echoed through the darkness. Followed by the sound of the animal running and jumping away, followed quickly by a couple more snorts.

He sat there for a moment, trying to stop his entire body from shaking. He even thought he could stay right there and not leave until it was daylight, but he was long past knowing how long that would be.

He slowly slipped around the tree, crawled up to his feet, and began to move again, trying to stay as quiet as possible.

He kept moving down the hill slowly, carefully crawling over underbrush where he could make sure every footfall was secure. The last thing he wanted to do was fall again or make any unnecessary noise. He traveled another ten minutes at a slow pace until he thought he could see the outline of an old house. He broke into a run when he felt his feet his gravel. He didn't stop until he reached the porch. He slid past the banister and didn't even try a knock as he grabbed the handle and twisted it, but it didn't open. No one answered. He placed his shoulder into the door, one quick hit, and it popped open. He quickly stepped inside and shut it behind him.

Chapter Six

Dustin slammed the door behind him with such force that dust, dirt, and he couldn't tell what else covered him over, causing him to cough.

"Hello," he muttered with no expectation of an answer.

There was extraordinarily little chance the old house was inhabited. He took a deep breath. He wanted to laugh but found nothing came out as he slid down the frame with his back firmly against it. All he wanted to do was sit there and wait for daylight. He would worry about everything else after he could see his surroundings. He would be safe when it was daylight out.

He sat there in the dark and just listened. The house creaked when the wind shifted outside. There were moments he almost thought he could hear footsteps somewhere above him, but when he looked up, all he saw was spiderweb.

"Amber," he muttered his fiancé's name. He took a long moment, thinking about her dark black hair and freckles that would make a redhead jealous of her. He felt his face flush with excitement.

"Hey, we really going to do this?" Amber questioned as she sat wearing nothing more than his t-shirt with his favorite football team's logo on the back. He couldn't help but stare at her exposed thighs just under the hem of the shirt.

"Are you having second thoughts?" he said, bouncing down on the bed beside her, feeling a spring from the old mattress stab him in the ribs, but that didn't stop him. He lowered his hand, placing them on the inside of her legs, and traveled upward until she rolled over into him. She was still looking at the ring on her finger.

"No… but this was too much," she said. The ring was red in color. It wasn't a diamond, though he didn't know exactly what type of stone it was. The only one he could afford.

"It's not too much. Nothing is ever going to be too much for you," he replied, pushing his arm under her and pulling her in close to him. "I love you."

"I love you," she answered, leaning in against him. "Have you told Jacob yet we're moving?"

"No, I'm going to do that tonight," he said, tugging her until she was sitting on his lap. He thought about tearing the shirt open, but then it was his favorite shirt. She shifted her weight, pushing herself into him back onto the bed. He pushed the hair out of her face, lost in her eyes.

Dustin sighed as he opened his eyes. He didn't even know if Jacob was alive or not. He looked at his boots, seeing something move. He turned the light on, shining on his overly worn boots. A small black spider with red markings sat on the tip of his boot, its long legs extended upward as if it was going to pounce on something. A black widow spider. He kicked his boot, and the spider disappeared into the darkness.

"Damn spiders," he huffed.

He took his time shining the light all around the room, and he counted twenty different spiderwebs littering the area. He looked to the ceiling above him once again. Half of the sheetrock was gone, and it was easy to see a big spiderweb there. As the light hit the web, a cluster of small dark and brown spiders scattered to escape the light. He glanced at his boot; the spider was back, this time threading around his laces. He quickly reached forward, smacking the webbing and the spider.

"Go away," he spat.

He finished removing all the webbing before pushing his way up to a standing position. Dustin took into the room from a standing position. He reached over to the nearby light switches and flipped both, and there was no response anywhere. He hadn't expected there to be. The home looked like it had spent a lifetime empty.

He walked over to the nearby bay window and pushed the curtains, feeling the spiderweb intertwined with his fingers as he did so. He peaked outside and saw no neighboring houses. He watched closely where he thought he had emerged from the darkness. He wasn't entirely sure it was where he had come down, but it had to be close enough. If there had been anything following him, he'd see it.

He turned to find an old recliner and pushed it over against the entrance door where he had been sitting a few minutes before. It wouldn't take much for something or someone to push it clear, but at least he would hear it if they did. The house didn't look that different from any other old settlement house in the area. The furniture was old, and the paint was peeling off the walls. One thing he did see that set it out was an old oak crown molding hung where the walls met the ceiling. Someone had spent money and time making it look like something out of an old Southern home. He imagined this house had been standing since the '50s or '60s, and though it was abandoned now, at one time, a large family spent time inside the walls.

He stepped around a corner, stopping at what used to be a kitchen area, and he could see a door leading to the outside. He quickly rushed forward to shut it. It caught on the floor as he pushed. He shoved his weight into it until it closed to the outside. He grabbed what used to be an old broom and pushed it in place, hoping it would help keep the door closed. He broke the long handle in half, keeping a part of it for himself. It was no shotgun or knife, but it would have to do.

He saw an old rotary phone. He quickly picked it up and hit the button. The only reason he knew how to work it was that his grandmother still had one hanging in her kitchen that he played with while growing up. He knew there would be nothing on the other end, but he had to try. He pulled his hand away, looked at the spiderweb that trailed behind and shook his hand to ensure it was all gone, especially what he didn't see. He was feeling the effects of seeing all the webbing. Whether he had any spiders on him or not, he felt them all over.

He shined the light all around and thought about the woman. Even if she looked like a woman, she was as much a spider, and he was starting to realize as he took in the kitchen. He might be in the spider's den, and a chill crawled up his back, causing him to shake.

He turned to look for anything that might be used as a weapon beside the broken broom, realizing that it may have been of little use to the spider creature. He found a kitchen knife in an old drawer, mostly rusted, but he realized quickly it was going to be his only other option. He stepped back into the living room, approaching the door as slowly as he could as the old wood under his feet creaked from age. Dustin pulled the old, raggedy curtain out of the window, looking all around the area. The floors above him creaked from weight as someone walked. It was on the roof or in an attic. He looked up as dust sprinkled down around him. He gathered his composure and took a deep breath. The creaking continued. He saw no access to the attic, even if there was one. He imagined that if he was in some sort of den. There was an access or hole somewhere for it to slip into the house. He ripped the curtain off the rod and covered the light. It shined dimly now, as he didn't want it to be so obvious. He skirted the edge of the wall until he reached the kitchen, glaring at the back door that had been opened before. He continued moving, his back to the wall as he passed by the kitchen until he came to what he thought was an old bedroom. He went from room to room, shining the light, looking for any other way out or, more importantly, any way that the creature could get in, and as he reached the last room, there was none. There was no access to an attic or massive hole for the creature to shimmy through. He slowly made his way back to the entrance to the house, stopping when he saw the door that he hadn't noticed before, opposite from where he entered the house. He shined the light on it. He glanced back at the entrance door. *He could make another run for it. It has to be getting close to daylight. An hour, two at the most.*

The last thing he wanted to really do was go back out into the dark with that creature waiting on the roof or somewhere nearby to pounce. He crossed the room to the door and put his hand on the knob, and hesitated. He quickly opened the door, shoving the point of the broken broomstick out into the darkness, but hit nothing but air.

He realized that the noise from the roof had stopped as he stared at the old staircase heading down into the darkness.

"Shit," he muttered to himself.

Click, click, click.

He took one step back, and his hand started to shake and tremble. He shined a light to the bottom of the stairs. The hand holding the broken broomstick rested on the door, ready to shut it. Though he couldn't see her, he knew she was there watching with her six red eyes. He saw movement in the shadows. Without hesitation, Dustin slammed the door shut, so hard plaster shook from the wall around the frame. He placed his back against the door. He held a tight grip on the knob and felt the pressure on the other side as it tried to turn, but he tightened his grip. He held it there tightly, trying to listen, but there were no sounds coming from the other side. The pressure from the other side continued to try to twist. Dustin gritted his teeth and kept his grip.

Dustin placed his back to the door; one hand firmly grasped the knob as he slid down into a seated position, where he closed his eyes and rested his head back against the wood structure. He tried to remember Amber's eyes from the morning before, but as he tried to concentrate, all he could see were the six red eyes staring back at him. He gave it a tap; it was a solid wood door, which made sense since it was an older house. The knob had stopped moving, but as he sat there, he could hear the slight wheezy breathing coming from the other side, so close he thought he could feel the creature's warm breath on the back of his neck.

"Please let me go," he said in no more than a whisper.

"You saw me," a small voice called from the other side. It wasn't so much of a whisper of a female voice from the other side. It was soft and hollow, sounding almost like it lay there echoing in his ear.

Click, click, click.

Obviously, a fingernail or something on the other side of the old wooden door. "Please," he pleaded a little louder than before. His heart seemed to stop as he waited for a reply.

"You saw me," she repeated in the same hollow tone.

"I won't tell anyone," he pleaded as he knocked his head back into the door.

The knob started turning forcefully. He turned, grabbing it with both hands, holding it steady, and his shoulder firmly pushed into the old wooden surface.

"Yes, you will. You have no choice; this is a world you can't unsee. I'm something you can't unsee…" Dustin thought about how this woman… this creature he saw in the woods, the eyes, the things protruding from her jaws, and he knew she was right. The door jarred from the other side. He imagined she had thrust into it.

Dustin looked at his hand. The knife was gone. It only took a moment to see it had slid away from him at some point. He reached for it, trying not to take his hand off the doorknob, his boot off the frame, but he couldn't quite reach. He glanced back at his hand and then at the knife. Two seconds was all he needed. He stretched, took his hand off the knob, and grabbed the knife. As he turned back, he heard the knob screech as it twisted. He lunged back in, grabbing the knob and placing his shoulder again. He shoved the knife into the door.

There was a squeak and then a rumble as something scurried away. His heart raced as he put his ear to the door and listened. He could hear a faint echo, a *click, click, click,* coming away from the door.

He gathered himself, took a big deep breath, stepped forward, and pulled a knife from the door. He kept a hand on the doorknob and looked at the red blood on the blade. "Human blood?"

He lowered himself to look through the hole where he pulled the knob. He saw a single red eye staring back at him. Dustin fell back from the door, losing the knife in the fall. They jerked away from the top of the frame but did not open completely. Plaster burst from around the door as it shuttered again from another hard thrust.

He placed his hand on the doorknob leading to the outside. It had to be getting close to daylight. He looked to the window, still seeing only darkness as another jolt came from the basement door, and stopped moving when he opened the door to the outside.

Dustin watched the door intently. One foot on the outside heard footsteps on the roof again. He stepped back in, pulling the large door shut on the frame, and latched it tight again. He stepped over to the window and slightly pushed the curtain away to look at the porch. He saw her there in a crotched position, sitting on the banister, looking directly at him, her red eyes distinct in the darkness of her face. It reminded him of a spider more so than ever, sitting, waiting for the prey to get caught in its web. His hand began to shake uncontrollably as her head shifted to one side.

Dustin turned back, looking at the basement door. She had moved so fast to the outside that there was possibly more than one. He turned to take another look at the porch, and she was gone. He knelt, trying to get a better look at the ceiling of the porch, thinking he would see her there above the window waiting, but there was nothing. He stood watching for a good five minutes until he felt the cool breeze on his neck. He hissed out anger as he left the curtain's fall. He stepped in the direction of the kitchen slowly, moving, thinking he would see her there standing, but what he saw after a moment was a wide-open door to the outside. He stepped away from the curtains, looking closely at the area around him and between him and the new opening. Out of the corner of his eye, he saw her. He slowly took a step back, watching as she seemingly glided from the ceiling gradually to a crouched position on the floor only a few feet away from him.

He turned without hesitation, rushed to the front door, opened it, and ran out, leaping from the porch, which was much further off the ground than he remembered. He twisted wrong and came up limping, heading down the gravel road. He could see more now; it was so close to daylight that he thought he could see the sun breaking over the horizon. He ran, mostly pulling his ankle along with him, and then he heard the scattering of gravel behind him.

Dustin turned; he would not die being attacked from behind. He twisted and fell onto his back, knocking the oxygen out of him. He rolled over, trying to get back up onto his feet, and he felt it. The cold feeling taking him and the searing pain of something being stuck into the soft tissue of his neck, and then he felt her weight on his back.

Chapter Seven

"I love you," she answered, leaning in against him. "Have you told Jacob yet we're moving?" She was so close he could feel the warmth coming off her skin. The smell of honeysuckle engulfed his senses. His heart raced as if something wasn't quite right.

"No, I'm going to do that tonight," he muttered, tugging closer against him until he could smell her skin, the sweet scent of honeysuckle... but Amber hated honeysuckle. He nestled into her neck, getting a better smell as his neck began to throb. Had she bitten him? He slowly pushed her away and looked up into her six red eyes.

Dustin woke. His heart raced as he tried to move, but there was no response from his paralyzed limbs. He was numb and weak, as if he had just woken up from a two-day binge drinking that he and his friend Jacob had all too often done in their youth.

He remembered Jacob and the horrified male screams he heard as he tried to get up, and his head started pounding. This was more than a hangover. He remembered the woman lowering herself down on top of him and the pressure on his neck. He took a long, deep breath. He couldn't move more than his head; the rest of his body didn't follow along. He struggled but didn't move any further than the moment before. He gasped for air, his mouth dry, and his throat throbbed. He tried to yell for help, but nothing came out, and through the headache, he felt the restraints on the rest of his body. It wasn't rope. It was something sticky and seemed to cover the entirety of his body. He didn't have to think long about the substance that was holding him. Web. He was encased in some sort of webbing. He gritted his teeth and twisted his entire body, pushing his right shoulder forward, and could hear it ripping until he could shift to look in the direction of the light he was seeing somewhere across the room. The light flickered; a single candle lit in the darkness. He took a deep breath, recognizing the same musty smell from the house, and he knew he was in the basement of the old, abandoned house.

"What do you want from me?" he whimpered.

Click, click, click.

The candle moved, raised in the air as if floating up and then across the room toward him. He realized then the creature was walking across the ceiling. He tried to focus using the light of the candle to get a better look, but he could never see more than movement in the shadows.

"Why?" he mumbled, unsure if he'd even made a noise.

The light from the candle again dropped as he watched the shadow emerge from the ceiling and drop down to the floor in a doorway he could see clearly now. Another candle lit, then a third and fourth until there was light all over the room in front of him. Dustin glanced down and saw the webbing holding him in place and the dried blood where the creature had bitten him on his shirt.

He glanced back up and could clearly see the silhouette of a woman before she entered the light. She circled around, lighting more candles with her back to him. He noticed her light strawberry-blonde hair. It was the woman from the woods. She moved with hesitation. Despite everything he thought he knew about her, she seemed less sure of herself with each step she took.

"Help me," he muttered, and she paused, her head slightly tilted, and her body twisted so that she could look back at him.

She was frowning, and for the first time, he could truly see her. Her face was sharp and narrow, with a slightly pointed nose and thin eyes that he couldn't make out the color. She didn't look anything like the creature he had seen in the woods. Her lips, tinted red, forced a smile, and he could see the place where the mandibles had come from her cheeks, still red from the painful metamorphosis. His neck started pulsating, and he remembered her biting him. There were no other eyes, just those glaring back at him. She was wearing only the slip of a robe that she was spilling out of; her breasts were firm with nipples that seemed hardened through the soft fabric, and his body reacted in a way that sent a cold chill down his back. Her hips were large, and her thighs. She was muscular. He could see this woman was forty to forty-five at the oldest. He would have called her beautiful if she hadn't scared him to death. Her smile went away when their eyes met. For a moment, she almost seemed human. Like she regretted what she had done or what she was about to do. The thought caused his heart to race as he struggled against the web.

"Please," he muttered, watching her circle around the room, getting closer with every step she took but never looking back at him. Dustin shoved his shoulder forward once again, and the webbing ripped further until he was able to pull his right arm free.

Click, click, click.

He glanced at the woman. She stood, facing him. He could see the hand resting on the table and a singular long fingernail clicking on the old rustic wood.

"Don't do this," he muttered. Her eyes were green and not the nightmarish red from before as she stared at him emotionlessly. There was a splash of lightly colored freckles on her face, exactly like her lightly colored hair. His eyes drifted down her body, his heart racing with such uneasiness as he took her in.

"Who are you?" he questioned, his eyes again meeting hers. The redness of her cheeks was gone completely now.

"Just a widow," she responded. Her voice was harsh, gravelly, not the sound he had expected, but the way she said it was more than an expression of having lost a love. It was the creature. The thoughts of the small black widow spider from the doorway above crossed his mind as her eyes narrowed.

The old ghost stories he had been told growing up flashed before him, tales of this holler, of a woman who would cannibalize her husband, and the stories that would haunt generations. "You can't be the widow," he said harshly. "You'd be nearly..."

"I'm much older," she stated, and a smile graced the corner of her mouth. And for a moment, he saw the flash of her bloody teeth before she quickly hid them again. She turned her back, and he started to try to pull his other arm free. He realized most of his body still was not responding, only the left side.

"The venom in your system has slowed the rest of your body from acting the way you want. I'm not sure if that ever goes away."

He knew what that meant. She had never let anyone live long enough to see if the numbness went away, but there was also a strange expression on her face as she looked down at her hand with the long fingernail.

"It works differently on men and women..." She paused as she glanced up at him. "You may not even feel the pain." He watched as she bit down on her lower lip, her eyes now a strange pinkish color, and her cheeks were flushed once again. Her voice grew shallower and more haunting as it neared a hiss. Her green eyes were gone now, looking more yellow in the firelight.

"What are you?" Dustin questioned.

"Old and tired," she hoarsely responded, a hand resting on her stomach and another on the table at her side where the candle now sat. It was obvious from her posture she was holding herself upright. He never even saw her set the candle down. A hand drifted down her body. He tried to look away but couldn't stop watching her. She seemed remorseful for what she had done, at least conflicted.

"I'm getting married in a week," he said in his calmest voice, though even he could tell he was stammering.

She dropped her head as if to look at the floor. He could see her mouth. The smile was gone and looked more like a frown. She never looked up to meet his eyes; she only shook her head no, and he knew she was answering his statement.

"I'm sorry" was barely more than a whisper as it carried on the wind.

"Ppplease," he pleaded.

Her lips parted as she dropped down to her knees and then fell back into a seated position.

"You don't have to do this," he continued to plead. She fell back onto her back and arched her stomach upward into the air. "I'm getting married. I'm supposed to be getting married. Please don't do this, please…"

He saw her head tilt, and her eyes, all six of them, glowed as she looked at him, blood red, with black veins traveling from one eye to the next. Her body contorted as she lifted herself up into a standing position using nothing but her legs with her back to him. The robe dropped down her arms, and he focused on her slender, attractive frame, knowing he had only had a few moments. Her fingernails matched the hideous black nail he had seen on only one finger earlier. Her body shifted with her head as she turned slightly to look at him. The long arthropods stretched wide from her cheeks, black, a stark difference to her pale face. As they came open, he shivered when he saw her distinct sharp teeth no longer hidden by her chapped, blistered lips.

The End

Milton Keynes UK
Ingram Content Group UK Ltd.
UKHW010809220424
441551UK00001B/96

9 798218 385026